MARGARET MAHY, the iconic author from New Zealand, who sadly died in 2012, wrote more than 200 books for children of all ages, and is acknowledged to be one of the outstanding authors of the 20th century. In 2006 she was awarded the Hans Christian Andersen Medal, which is the highest international recognition granted to authors and illustrators of children's books. Twice winner of the Carnegie Medal, several of her books have become modern classics. Her picture books for Frances Lincoln include *Dashing Dog*, with Sarah Garland, and *Down the Back of the Chair* and *Bubble Trouble*, both illustrated by Polly Dunbar.

POLLY DUNBAR studied Illustration at Brighton College of Art, and now lives and works in Brighton. She is the internationally acclaimed author and illustrator of *Penguin*, *Dog Blue* and the *Tilly* books. Her picture books for Frances Lincoln include *Looking After Louis* and *Measuring Angels*, both written by Lesley Ely, as well as *Down the Back of the Chair* and *Bubble Trouble* with Margaret Mahy.
www.pollydunbar.com

9 39846240

To Roxy and Riley – P.D.

JANETTA OTTER-BARRY BOOKS

Text copyright © Margaret Mahy 2012
Illustrations copyright © Polly Dunbar 2012

The right of Margaret Mahy to be identified as the author of this work,
and of Polly Dunbar to be identified as the illustrator of this work, has been asserted by them
in accordance with the Copyright, Designs and Patents Act, 1988 (United Kingdom).

First published in Great Britain in 2012 by
Frances Lincoln Children's Books,
74-77 White Lion Street, London N1 9PF
www.franceslincoln.com

First paperback published in Great Britain in 2013

All rights reserved

No part of this publication may be reproduced, stored in a retrieval system, or transmitted, in any form, or by any
means, electrical, mechanical, photocopying, recording or otherwise without the prior written permission of the
publisher or a licence permitting restricted copying. In the United Kingdom such licences are issued
by the Copyright Licensing Agency, Saffron House, 6-10 Kirby Street, London EC1N 8TS.

A catalogue record for this book is available from the British Library.

ISBN 978-1-84780-474-7

Set in Heatwave

Printed in China

3 5 7 9 8 6 4 2

THE MAN
FROM THE LAND OF
FANDANGO

Margaret Mahy

Polly Dunbar

F
FRANCES LINCOLN
CHILDREN'S BOOKS

The man from the land of Fandango

Is coming to pay you a call.

With his tricolour jacket and polka-dot tie
And his calico trousers as blue as the sky

And his hat with a tassel and all.

And he bingles and bangles and bounces,

He's a bird! He's a bell! He's a ball!
The man from the land of Fandango
Is coming to pay you a call.

Oh, whenever they dance in Fandango,
The bears and the bison join in,

And baboons on bassoons make a musical sound,

And the kangaroos come with a hop and a bound.

And the dinosaurs join in the din.

And they tingle and tongle and tangle

Till tomorrow turns into today.

Then they stop for a break and a drink and a cake

In their friendly fandandical way.

The man from the land of Fandango

Is given to dancing and dreams,

He comes in at the door like a somersault star

And he juggles with junkets and jam in a jar

And custards and caramel creams.

And he jingles and jongles and jangles

As he dances on ceilings and walls,

And he only appears every five hundred years

So you'd better be home when he calls.

MORE FANTASTIC PICTURE BOOKS BY MARGARET MAHY AND POLLY DUNBAR FROM FRANCES LINCOLN CHILDREN'S BOOKS

DOWN THE BACK OF THE CHAIR

"The entertainment, humour and exuberance of it all arises from what Dad finds – down the back of the chair! Mahy's text rollicks along and Polly Dunbar's graphics are akin to a fireworks display on the page" – *School Librarian*

"Exuberant rhyming story celebrating the chaos of everyday life and the power of the imagination" – *Independent on Sunday*

"The language really fizzes!" – *Daily Telegraph*

BUBBLE TROUBLE

"A huge adventure with laugh-out-loud text and gorgeous illustrations" – *Lovereading*

"A joy to read aloud" – *Bookseller*

"Never fails to delight" – *The Times*

Frances Lincoln titles are available from all good bookshops.
You can also buy books and find out more about your favourite titles,
authors and illustrators on our website: www.franceslincoln.com